Anansi

DISCARDED

pearl

pearl

poems

Lynn Crosbie

Published in 1996 by
House of Anansi Press Limited
1800 Steeles Avenue West
Concord, Ontario
L4K 2P3
Tel. (416) 445-3333
Fax (416) 445-5967

Canadian Cataloguing in Publication Data
Crosbie, Lynn, 1963-
Pearl

Poems.
ISBN 0-88784-578-9

PS8555.R61166P43 1996   C811'.54   C96-930622-9
PR9199.3.C76P43 1996

Printed and bound in Canada

*House of Anansi Press gratefully acknowledges the support of the Canada
Council and the Ontario Arts Council in the development of writing and
publishing in Canada.*

Contents

For Sophia —

Goddaughter & Pearl-Girl

those i knew
shared with or loved   for those

whose absence was tangible almost real
something opened inside shattered
i was culpable it was personal
this implicated me   where i'm from

— Michael Holmes

I am nothing else and cannot be anything else
I am nothing but a mass of spikes going through me

— Franz Kafka

Pearl

Ande precious perles unto his pay.
             Amen, Amen.

Valentine, bishop of Interamna waited for execution in his cell
this February. Heart-shaped florets arrayed on his desk —
the Lupercalian festival. Winter,

cold spider-nevi, misting his window-glass.

He had shaved his head into a smooth pearl some months earlier.
The last time I saw him I looked away. His delicate scalp,
the low, menacing whistle, afraid of him.

> I thought he was powerful because of his contempt,
> his anger. His silk-yellow hair, sheared; I had
> wanted to touch this

sleek daffodil, once. His eyes are seawater; their calm blue surface belies
what is beneath — fire-coral, stingrays.

> I saw water on his kitchen floor and called out anxiously
> to him, I thought you were dead, I thought you were dead.

Dressed in red on Valentine's Day — crimson ribbons, lips, and bows,
      I answer the telephone:
John is dead, I'm sorry, he killed himself last night.

I walk to his apartment and climb the stairs. The hallway is
      sweet smelling,
cloying; his door is in flames, prohibiting entrance.

I will see him again, and again.

At the morgue — his mottled face arched against the metal frame,
      only his forehead is recognizable.
A pale expanse, it looks like bliss, as smooth as stone.

And in dreams — he kisses me with awkward passion; he is telling me
     what he has found.
He was so uneasy, with gestures, with love: *The thought of having
     close friends frightens me.*
I never touched him, I gave him roses instead.

The way that roses die, their scarlet flush betrayed by the careless sepal. The
thorns provide little protection, the thorns

like the bowl of water, offer a half-life: they are dead already.

His rooms already vacant, empty datebooks, a small framed photograph
     of Yukio Mishima:
Beauty, beautiful things . . . those are now my most deadly enemies.

          His pink knit blanket strewn on the floor, the depressions
          in the pillows. A ring of tiny keys, an empty vial:
          I have taken 45–50 Ativan, I did not plan to write this letter.

I think of the plastic shroud intoxicating him, his breath becoming
narcotic; there is nothing here. In the absence, of regret and menace,
I gather his suicide detritus and seal it in a paper bag

where I have entombed his last answering-machine message: *I haven't
     talked to you in a while,*
call me.

He asks that his notebooks be burned — the fire that has now erased him,
tissue, marrow, bone, unfolding, a whisper, *I did not plan to*

I find that he has forgiven me, too late. An outline in his notes
(there were folders, flat, unrequited desires) plots a story
where I appear with an electric guitar and a strange fit,
of prescience:

* *The time she came to my apartment and saw water on the floor & thought I was dead.*

The memories and affections he buried, frail green shoots in fallow
    underground. Lost
in ineffable misery, *he turns once more*, to what is left.
    Heartbreak —
two tattered slippers, a window with a view of asphalt, metal stairs.

His lustrous head in its oyster shell — he rattles as he surrenders
    an obscure ghost.
I have never been religious, his spirit enters strangers, machines,
    a photograph.

Taken as I watched, a summer morning, I thought, for the first time,
    he was beautiful.
Serene and knowing — grey clouds have descended on this still frame,

clouds portending

I will call you, many times — sometimes I will berate you, *my partner
in crime,* and sometimes I will ask you
to take me with you.

Nine Hammer Blows
for Kenneth Halliwell

John, we used the language as if we made it

— Robert Lowell

People don't like to be told
that you're sick
and then be forced
to watch
you
come
down
with the hammer.

— Anne Sexton

a deliberate form of frenzy — John, who sleeps so easily, and I,
setting out barbiturates, grapefruit juice: *If you read his diary all will*
be explained. Especially the latter part, I wrote,

and crushed his skull with nine hammer blows. He is still warm when
    I lie down.
My eyes closing, I see blood on the Magdalene, the mandolin, my design —

it has come to this. The latter part — eight pages — has disappeared,
    the diary ends
and what, what became of us in early August. It was painfully bright;
    I do not care
what others think and pause at the spiked-black entrance gate,

drawing its points across my throat. You're sick, he says and leaves,
    more often these days, or
presses a napkin to the telephone. I hear murmured devotions, *soon, patience*
my love —

he loved me once, that I was sick, the things I saw. Spider monkeys in
roses, a ladder of cat's heads.

sometimes I love poverty, a friend wrote; I miss everything.
I was the first

to explain tragedy to him *(not wisely but too well)*, to lubricate
my fingers and
open him, tenderly easing the petals of the rosette, my tongue in his
urethra, a taste of honey

much sweeter than wine, music, slipping between our single beds to kiss
and the slow sedative
caress. The poppy is the first bloom I place on the walls, radiant, it
pollinates the field

I attend with my paste and scissors. I do not have his facility with
words, the orderly entries, dated,
detailed. The scent of cherry, urinal stones, the cup of a stranger's hand
on his balls,

my orchids. I iron his briefs and pillowslips, trying to smoothe the
disorder, sheer terror is all I feel,
and the walls become heavy with paradise, marble gods recast, the
choir invisible, angels striking

Moroccan princes. We were so still in the sand I thought we may
never rise, the funereal
smoke of *kif* burning in censers, yellow-shirts embalming us with their
religious lips.

I was his shadow, paling behind him a little cloud. The hammerclaws
leave two impressions
on my palm. That he cannot leave me, so much is lost already (slivers
of paper, haloes, shields),

how necessary shadows are. The fastened grey shape that retreats in
pursuit, that may precede you.
Revealing your presence, gesturing to the distance of the sun,

I had to remove my clothing as I fell to my knees. Dying, you were still able
      to produce antiphony,
red flares of blood shining in the eclipse, the yellow fire in me.

Close to you I try to touch you, I see eight sheets fall like linens, like spirits.
As immaterial as purity, as sacred as the shadows

that seek me and falter, erased in the flames, a disclosure —

We went to bed early. Kenneth was looking wan.

Monday 31 July 1967.

I've Got You (Under My Skin)

just the thought of you makes me stop before I begin

Le Comte and I meet in discreet little corners to tender the tripled
    envelope and *chevaux-de-frise*,
skin-popping — unseen ormolu emblems, the lips of goddesses devised
    below the metal tines.

Perhaps it is hatred that lures me to these ravines or alleys, or the beguiling feel
of the long sleek rats making anklets of their tails. Casting shadows
in the blue night, he sails a fleet of gauze dressings

in the grey water that eavesdrops at our feet. And we visit restaurants
    in disguise;
my Cleopatra hair *comes undone* when he compares each violet
    tendril to ivy,
coronating the sun. Veils of ivy, the moon's black lashes

sweep its sweet yellow face, I am somewhere slow. Delicately he
    retrieves his pocket knife,
and in half circles of light stabs the spaces between my fingers.
I do not flinch, even as its reckless edges bite

accented initials, a monogram, in the folded linen napkins: *notre lune
    de miel*, my Count's
mouth is pursed, a scarlet stain, a memory of choke cherries, longing to taste

this poison, its red allure. Mars refracted, rubies pendant in gathers
    of Nile

silk is his look, lids lowered over jade-green eyes.

Folded like Japanese lanterns, *ancient oceans*, they draw me in.
    Easier to breathe beneath these
paper pagodas,

he dreams of mutilation:

> O, *how sweet it is to snatch some child brutally*
>
> *from his bed*
>
> *to plunge your long nails into his soft breast*

and then you drink the blood.

Because of its science and purity, sun-bleached fossils, the scorpion in resin, a matrix of colourless cells.

I look at the pale nimbus of his hair (the clouds that smother the sky) without apprehension.
My *ecstasy gone underground*, a cool white stone, and his ear, pressed to mine, is a pink shell

Purplish Semele, I can almost hear the music. Whales moving in pods, their arias of love, the simplicity.
Of seawater on flesh, of motion, graceful, unconscious.

Bliss, that sinks under the points of spears; they colour the sea with their descent

and I count each fall, I watch his pallid face as we come down into despair,

familiar to us — we practice deception and we have obligations, promises to keep. Addiction is paramount,
the mainline, the *ethic of closeness*,

that is only consecrated when the needle enters,
and retrieves its taste of blood.

The Balcony

The sun's a thief and with his great attraction
Robs the vast sea. The moon's an arrant thief,
And her pale fire she snatches from the sun.

— *Timon of Athens*

Cyril — *the sallow picture of my poisoned love* — is a stranger
and a thief. His urchin eyes terrify; once, I traced their
spokes and shadows, a catch in his voice I mistook for rapture.

A night of broken glass, the burnished lights were honeycombs,
fireflies; a pale fire burned lightly

his kiss is calculated, as hot and practised as the sun.

We stood on the balcony looking past the sliver of sea. His hands
spread like starfish to gather the fabric of my sleeves.

I remember a jellyfish bite, its scarlet geography.
Surprised by danger, I look away.

I am almost unconscious — the Neptune-blue analgesics provide
an armature, a borrowed green garter, *with gold overwrought*.

Crimson fins and coral sway seductively against my ankles;
there is life under water, my veins are leafstalks

nourishing the hyacinths and lilies.

Pain, his great attraction. He asks me to slap his faultless face,
to slice the cardinal scar that divides his ribcage.

I sink my teeth into his neck and extract a bruise
yellow, ochre — it is this he remembers, when he writes to me, and
     nothing else.

I have nightmares: a bullet in my heart, a formation of brownshirts,
a boy who stalks me, who creeps into my bedroom at night. His face is
livid and I approach him:

Let me wash the blood from your beautiful face.

(Of suicide I often think)

That I would drift that day, through the metal slats. The cherry-blossoms
falling in sweet coronets, ardent only for this.

The pang of his voluptuous lips, a supplement

A covenant I honoured, when I wrote him — there are white birds,
    beating against my window,
orange chalk on the ledge, spelling your name — he who is (like) God.

He is a sensual conduit for the sublime, for the faith and beauty
    I surrendered this spring.

I seal this letter with perfume: *My Sin*. I do not hear from him again,
silence envelops me like a silken net,

the brilliant lures, sharp hooks of memory.

He told me he was born in the year of the Tiger. Black and gold stripes,
that signal peril, where there is no language.

Where there is only an uneasy sense; viciousness, stalking patiently
in the grass and leaves. Your gentle touch, tracing the lips
of marigolds, the soft pads of the cat's paws.

Without dismay you accept the sting, the ravaging claws that sever
your throat; you are quiet, as you must be.

You recede, like the tide, diminishing as the sun sinks into its still centre.

Its brightness eclipses, something as intangible as grace,

rapture, mathematical and precise. As certain as the veil of thorns,
the linen shroud, your eyes closing wearily, in death.

Have Gun, Will Travel

This is not vanity.
  Here error is all in the not done,
all in the diffidence that faltered.

— Ezra Pound

after Pam Grier

The mailbox at the foot of the stairs is tenantless; there is one Jesus
pamphlet — his arms outstretched, gesture. The depressions in his
    hands, bereft.

Moths circle the metal slot like gossamer, a skein of moths.

My own letters, vanished, unspeakable confessions: blackmail —
fields of iris — love retracting its yellow claws.

I have fewer friends. Tired of heartbreak, they avert their eyes,
    what have you done to yourself?
An incision, an accident: I have been impressed by his ardour,
    a memory of crescents, faint in the receding sky.

He loves me. I suffer his silence, its needles and pins, with pleasure.
    This is not vanity: the
Carmelite nuns that pass me on the street, their heads bowed, his arched collar,
    his vows, piety,

nausea. A terrible song *It must be him, it must be him*. Reason occluded,
    a quarter sun in the dark field of spirits.
If stars assemble in language, clouds replicate the plush
    sphere of his mouth,

it must be him. I am dressed in my starched nurse-whites, the simple
    gown and three-cornered
hat, a red cross. As I place my cool blue lingerie, my hot-pink peignoir in a
    portmanteau,

this little gun of metal and pearl.

He confided in me that he was afraid of murder, poison, suffocation —
    he wanted me to feel

dangerous. Secure that he may reserve his affection, the promises he
    breaks: I will see you soon,
I meant to write, I think of you often.

How pleased he will be when I surprise him with the cool barrel,
    when it arouses his neck, his temple.
Its sight lowers to the silver zipper, its cold teeth clenched,
    closed to me

anxious for the hot kiss of lead, hollow points of fear and trembling.

I want to excite him this way. His loneliness lost as the razor emerges
    from its sheath —
The long shining tail of the comet

that lights the sun in its orbit of ice.

There will be disarray, the inevitable blood I attend with bandages
    and stitches; it flows
unstopped because my evening shoes are insensible, hard red alligator,

without comfort — in love there are certain contracts we are bound
    to honour.

I will open his eyes with the edge of my leather gloves and there,
    in the quiet white orbits, there is the moon,
that crept between us, still, in its membrane of shadows,

the promises the night remembers, and obeys.

Superfly

Make your mind what you want it to be.

— Curtis Mayfield

Tired of waiting for him, I think of a plan to stick it to the
Man — he waylaid me with promises: protection, his valuable keys.
Nights of seduction, I would glide to the curb in my customized Eldorado,
black finish and cool bubble top

and turn it over to a superyoung girl with rags and a bucket of soapy
water, with a smile and a dead president, *make it shine my sister.*
He is inside listening to Curtis, his sapphire ring

he brings the moon with him, this cat, and his eyes glow like
mellow stones at my superfly threads. The cashmere white-stitched suit,
the maxi-coat trimmed in fox fur: *vixen,*

my pretty little hat with three blue feather plumes. I let him dig me
        for a while,
and lay a kiss, a spoon of cocaine on him, our secret meetings
a potent rush and I am hip to the hit to his fly hand on my thigh,

my ladies scatter in a cloud of Opium and he tells me,
you know me, I'm your friend.

I thought he was my man — I flash on him in the bathtub, its ledge of
        oils in flasks,
pulling a loofah sponge over my tired shoulders, passing a reefer
        in lemon paper,

on all the tired bitches working his keys, hustling his diamond rocks —
two sets of false eyelashes, micro-minis, freezing their asses off.

My .25 Beretta can't stop him, it's not real, I'm not real to him. He'll
use me up and kill me; I need brains guts and cool;
I put *fur* on your back, my baby, he says.

I am between him and death, *the greatest high of all*, and I ask him
    to step outside.
The pink flakes blow my mind and I turn to him with a flurry
    of karate kicks,
kicking out my left leg I bring him to the ground

and with my foot on the collar of his mohair suit I tell him, I took your
money and signed a contract on you: *I hired the best killers there are —*

men like you — *yeah, if one hair on my gorgeous head is harmed, it's
    all over for you.*
It's all over for you, I think, as I imagine I am Superfly; my mind is
    what I want it to be,
the Man is tired and suddenly he looks

old, very, very old as he turns away from me, the things he cannot dream —
my brazen plans, my *body full of love*.

Submission

for Mark and Debra: *Malleus Maleficarum*

The ground was never recovered, nor the legions, for their numbers were
thought so ill-omened that they never again appear in the army lists.

— J. M. Roberts

It begins with Diane — the gold shingles of her razored hair
alight in the wind that whips the trees,
the cotton slips pinned to nylon lines: these improbable ghosts.

The first I ever loved can still incite such desperation. Betrayal
lashes the careful stitches, the slight fabric;
its design undone.

She would take her switchblade and cut spiders in half —
a quadrant of scars radiating from her wrists and elbows, she wrote
      my name in blood,
let matches flare against the cuts

small yellow head, searing. I used to operate on myself, she said.
Separate a triangle of skin and place objects — silver pin
heads, glass beads — close to the bone.

A private surgical kit, embroidery scissors, alcohol, fine needles, and
violet thread; silk, cat whiskers tied in complicated bows. She
remembers this way, where things are

where they are buried. We studied history together, this is how we
      met. Recovering the Roman
Empire; she draws military disasters in her margins, mail-clad
      horsemen pitching
violently to the ground, the movement of the cavalry

a swarm of locusts. Her silver compact slit open, because there are
    assassins in the narrow hallway;
her fine pale feet turn to form an arabesque (a delicate
    design of flowers,
leaves), furrows in the sheets and mattress,

pearls. Ropes of black pearls and a black rubber dress — submerged in
    the green haze,
the depths of a nightclub, listening. *Submission*; she hit his thighs
    with a chain, a hook in his mouth

her lips were alluring. Red feather-quills, bright red flies. I think of
    him, brought violently
to the surface, his tensile body still below the thin edge of the filleting
    knife
his slick flesh streaming as he surrenders — a ceremony of scales and
    gills, useless to him now,

as he breathes in and out. She told me once that she was like a
    scorpion, and I did not listen.
I let her creep between my fingers, and danger was exotic to me then. I lived
    somewhere deep
beyond the coastline, in the crevices of rocks and wood-planks,

her gold hair spins like loose coins, strange and valuable. The
    currency of nightmares, where
the sun burns the earth and empties the seas — there are skeletons, gingerly
    reaching for night

night will fall in a rustle of wings, the gentle sweep of the legs of
    scorpions.

Radiant Boys

for Stephen McDougall (1962–1982)

there are legends of Radiant Boys, the apparitions of a young boy
usually surrounded by a glowing light or flame.

— Daniel Cohen

What was a cause for fear, doubt is now swept aside

— Horoscope, December 15, 1978

O the day I heard that, that he was dead — a panel truck at midnight,
    they identified
him by his teeth, arrowheads in the lattice-grille. He had been dead
    for years, to me.

My earliest ghost — the heat he emanated *(diving into the wreck)*;
    I tormented him
with adoration, stealing his ephemera, a flannel square, his shaky
    signature razored from a textbook.

He was painfully shy, his head nestled in his collarbone, with defiant eyes:
he lived on the other side — visiting his family's house in secret, I tore
dead stalks of grass, ragweed from the edges

where the lawn's decay kisses the street, I kiss

this strange bouquet, green fever spikes, my allergy to love. He would
    look at me, unsure,
his name written on my hands, my diffidence. Measuring the steps
    to his locker, his tree-fort,

he brought girls there with cherry wine, he called out their names
    — not mine.

And turning my own head away from him, terrified.

The soft skirt I bought, the colour of pumpkins. *Love's Baby Soft*
    blotted here
and there — embalm your wrist and throat in sweet pink, preserve
    this night.

There was a dance and I stood outside and saw him, apart from everyone,
dealing bags of grass. I watched the lights play *Stairway to Heaven* on
    his brass ring,
and he pulled me away to the bridge, *get higher baby,*

don't ever come down. He snaked his slender arms around me and
    scraped
his face against my hair, wanting to lick my lips, his hands lost in the
    supple orange,
the glow: *I try to talk to you and you won't look at me,*

I would not look at him then. Lost in his radiance and refusal,
    walking through fire,
luminous particles. The astrology that coursed beneath us: we turned
from the water, he turned to someone —

take care of her.

There is more and less: I came to meet him in an orchard and we bent
    together, bruised apples,
his tongue inquiring, what I could not offer.

Little stories — he washed his cat with Ivory soap, he left school early;
    he loved a girl.

Later, when I was far away, he told a friend: I know she is beautiful
    now, I can imagine this.

I found his death in an old newspaper — he had been trying to go
home. I never knew him, but speak to him still.

An apparition in a flame of light — he has things to tell me, that he
    reached out, beyond the
circle of his own angry reticence, to surround me, the first time anyone

tried to minister the chills (how coldly I hated myself), to divine — that
I would live, imagining his beauty,

loving this radiant boy.

I Hate Myself and Want to Die

Lately, I've become accustomed to the way
The ground opens up and envelops me . . .

Things have come to that.

— Amiri Baraka, "Preface to a Twenty Volume Suicide Note"

An arm, severed at the elbow, still aches. It becomes a phantom
limb, stirring without motion. Its ghost-fingers meet the air, on impulse;
there are sounds beneath the sea.

the dolphin has the power of hearing but no ears, signals
suspended in shirtsleeves and coral reefs, fissures in the surface
of the earth, danger and disbelief.

I am with Sarah, who rarely smiles, who suddenly covers her mouth
when a man with cauliflower hands passes by

I'm sorry, I always laugh at deformity, I don't know what's wrong. And
I think of my own mutation, like his,

but hidden — *Gloria* the dying plant beside me. Each day I pick
     another yellow leaf,
and return it to the bowl. A counterpane of fallen grief; it persists,
     stretching for the sun,
but the roots are bad, obscured

and tangled in shadows.

          Lately, I've become accustomed to the way
          the branches divide

          my actions from the urgent tide of longing, gratified
          by carelessness, a cut a bruise a fracture,

hate is the diagram unseen, words that stick like
splinters of ice, memories
that are becoming, to me.

I am being pushed to the ground and will not move, when someone
    intercedes
he says she's too ugly to feel pain, tries to break

my bones, but does not succeed. There are boxers in my family, their
    golden gloves shine when
I am battered and still reaching for the ropes.

My lips split, like the lacuna between bone and tissue, between what
    I can and cannot do:
I see that girl, lonely, despising herself

and forcing the days, the sun will rise and set *I am still alive,*

beside Gloria — this plant was once ripped from its earth and
    discarded (he was that angry at me).
There is little green in my touch; I patted the soil as if burying her.

This was years ago, she's still alive, exiling the yellow leaves and
    somehow, creating new
and fragile blooms, herself in miniature.

They look like the beautiful hands, misshapen, spectral, that are
    speaking to the light,
and listening to its sympathy, its silent response.

Paul Teale, Mon Amour

*My story is a love story, but only those tortured by love
can understand what I mean.*

— Martha Beck

Before you were apprehended you learned to calculate
statistical averages,
        that two and two would recur at random, I too
matriculate. Blonde on blonde, the malevolent look of love.

I called out to you as they folded you into the armoured car,
my letters secreted to your cell and examined
by censorious guards,

who are heartless and not divine.

You convey your affection with static hands, the demotic of the manacles
the metal links that mediate when I flush each night,
it is like a fever

when your innocent limbs collide with mine, your tender ministrations.
Combing the tangles from my hair, there are scissors placed safely
    behind you,
anaesthetizing me; your endearments enter the fragile tissue

the soft vistas of my wrists and elbows, drawing blood. And you
    draw tremors
on my spine with surgical intention, a theatre of lariats and silver
    duct-tape,
silver is the crown

that compels my silence. I am on my knees, subject to the
    choreography of zippers,
arcane briefs;

you have entered me, the song of angels in my sleep, such pretty girls.
I say that we are meant for each other, because you are blameless,
     your sweet
face an act of contrition, and I

petition for your release, and ask you to see. A room of velvet
     pillows, rich red wine,
opera, solitude. Cruel images hidden under your ties and laces; I will
     be stern, and
forgiving,

men have such obscure desires. Just look at his eyes, as untroubled, as
     clear as the sea that rages
in me; I will confess then, in the shadows of our secret evenings, you are
     not a stranger.
If you are kind to me, there is nothing else.

Their pristine bodies, helpless beneath saws and bindings that are not
     apocryphal,
the shock of flowers on their graves, my delight. Since you have
     spared me, I am singular —
remotely delicate,

your own duplicate, a killer without conscience, with an appetite that
     even you and your vicious
longings cannot requite.

The Snake Pit

for Tony

I know the purity of pure despair

— Theodore Roethke

He is often tired this fall, his eyes — purple shadows,
narcotic flowers. Glassine bags, black envelopes, ill-concealed secrets
I discover, sunflower dust, faint streaks of powder.

His horror of water, its purity and the sweetness he desires;
his mouth is burnt sugar, a honeycomb
where gorgeous insects recline.

I am afraid of anger, exhaustion: I'm just tired, my mother would say,
     as she
retreated to her bed; she would not speak for days. James sleeps
     and wakes
in strange furies: *you've never loved me, you wish I could take you places*

into the water, his body washing to the shore wreathed in seaweed
     and fire-coral.
Beyond recognition, he lies, and I believe him. Because I have my
     own secrets,

the same sweet tooth, the blue dissolution, a desire for serenity. When
the world is too much with me, and I revile myself,

forget to breathe. The first time I met him, shooting stars, once, twice,
my veins recoiled from the needle: *is this what you want?*

I wanted to retreat, to see beautiful things — the scars on his wrists,
our dishevelled hair, the cracks in the tiles — transformed;

he once lived by the water, collecting dead flowers and fish bones. He
     came to me with nothing,
and never left. We began to assemble these things together.

Broken elemental objects, as mysterious in origin as he, as the
     painting he made,
where he levitates above me, dormant and formless,

I'm just tired, he said, and disappeared. Later, there is a call; he has
        been institutionalized,
a breakdown. I visit him often, finding him in the long antiseptic corridors,
in the ice of his prim white bed.

We listen to someone play the piano — *some say love, it is a river*,
        I kiss him,
and ask him to get better. At night, he combs the winter streets for
        heroin, and sinks deeper
into the glacial corners of his sheets.

When he finds his way through the bleak cold he sees something
        growing — a fast seedling,
unattended, irreducible. It is as trite and as ravishing as the tentative music,
that played for us,

the seed, *that with the sun's love*, in the spring,

becomes the rose.

Condition

(of Louis Longhi: *the shampoo-killer*)

*Ladies and Gentlemen, we will not start with postulates but with an
 investigation.*

— Freud, Introductory Lectures on Psychoanalysis

My condition begins in silence and stealth, prowling from salon to
 salon, stealing their
instruments. Clips and pins, wire rollers, foil sachets of shampoo and
 hot oil: *extreme unction.*

I lay with my arms crossed over my white smock, a garland of scissors
 and tongs.

In the institution I would lock myself away, excising strands of hair
 from soap cakes, from the
mouths of drains. Long red tendrils, white strands —

black cilium. Examining their roots under glass, the fertile bulbs, their
 fibrous shoots.
The tulips I planted with my father in plots of snow; his head was
 light in the winter sun,
untouchable.

They grew in rows, snail plaits — *shine, softness, and manageability*;
 I required this alone,
at first. That the hair must lie on its velvet pincushion like
 a diamond, that
certain strands must be placed

in the open doorway between my room and the dark corridor, where
 hairdressers pass in rubber gloves
and tinting aprons — their irons glowing hot, beguiling me

to the call. I never harmed them, the first girls — I arched their necks
 into bowls of steaming
water, and lathered their hair with lemon juice, sage soaked in cider vinegar,
 herbs I grew in window boxes,

my hands pulling clouds through these tresses. Replenishing
     the follicles and cells
from my germinal garden (the rosehip of their dresses).

The *hair ceremonial* that ended with Marie — I had set and combed
     her hair,
listened to its clean squeak when I stretched it into rat's tails and
     coronets. I was afraid and tied
her to a chair, gagged her, scared she may refuse.

To submit to further care — there are certain ways of doing things —
     I could not stand to think
of her tangling and distressing the locks, splitting the ends

of the slipknots. I washed her hair until there was no more shampoo,
     and then, in a delirium
I know is love, I continued with honey, detergent, witch-hazel,
     bleach as she struggled

she tightened the ropes, my grip tightened and she strangled to death.
I hid her in the earth *stricken with remorse* the earth where
we set out the dull bulbs that would be tulips, switches of satin,
     yellow forelocks.

My father's head was covered with a golden down I longed to touch —
     when I reached out
with my child's fingers, he slapped them away.

I think of Marie, her uncovered skeleton, often. More often I trace
     the forbidden contours of the crown.

In my dreams the baby tigers are gentle — they cling to me
as I stroke them, they tender me their warmth.

My Soul

kiss kiss kiss kiss kiss — my soul

Mary's mother killed herself in late October, on a night of spirits, malevolent
witches. She lowered the blinds and in a pentacle of candles, carved a cross in her
chest — to capture him, his voice a hiss,

calling her to violence (haloes burn on Mary's wrists). She has saved
what papers remain:

soap, honey, napkins, *in itself weariness has something sickening about it,*
royal jelly, rat poison.

My own mother's operatic rage — her rage for order: there is a tissue on the floor,
my life is a ceaseless nightmare, *I lived for love*, and so on.

Locked in her room, dreaming of hangers aligned perfectly on wooden rods — I think
of pigeons, equidistant on my clothesline, in the revenant harmony

that women, looking backwards, desire.

She breaks storms with her tears, her faltering admission: *I can't do anything right.*
I would kill for her then, kill anyone who ever hurt her,

myself. The knife buried to the hilt, *I lived there, Mary, although I wrote unhappy* —
she keeps these papers in a metal box; she has come to hate memory.

This last October — Mary arrives, with a green witch-doll, an alligator
bag, her latest schemes.
She will make candelabras jewelled in rubies, pewter lamps
inlaid with tigers,

filigree skirts that catch the moon.

Her beautiful face clouds as she imagines a purity she does not
        disclose, something as lush,
as rare as the vines that encircle her face, the rubyfruit of her lips,
the Nile arches she paints over each eyelid.

Still, we are related through memory, years of altercation, accidental sister,
my soul. When the spirits descend this time, it is terminal. We
        withdraw from each other in
obscure anger, no longer able

to razor-cross the cobra's kiss, to drink its venom. Her slender
        hand raises, at half-mast,
as she walks away. Never to return,

I am complicit, her love a complicated blessing, and mine. A moment,
        unbidden, of women who
call upon malice, who entice injury, abnegation.

Our sleek black dresses, discarded on a stranger's chair, as we dance
        for him. Oblivious to his longing,
we plunged into the night until there was only silver,
        the line of silver below the sky —

remote and ancient, it swallows the ephemera, and separates us, the
        spokes of the sun,
retreating from its fierce centre.

The Fly

Where we almost, nay more than married are.

— John Donne

Pearl egg of fly intimates the curve of larva, its spine and claw-point.
    The cellophane shell,
brittle pupa-blanket where the almost fly

lies like a spring. Coiled and tensile, its exertions will tear the sheet.
    Six black legs flutter
against the dry christening gown, I see his lambent eyes

cloistered in these living walls of jet.

Small glider, his veined wings are sheer parasols, gauzy skirts that
    admit the light. The orange
down of his pelvis beneath this architecture, blood is the adhesive

fastening flight, my sleek aviator presses his sucker feet to my lips.
    How little
he denies me, the drone in my ear and he swarms my heart if one

two light steps from the tips of my fingers he bows his head and
    makes a violin,

or hovers behind me when I circle the floor, lonely, he rests on
    shoulder, elbow, to
stare at me with swollen eyes,

darkling, drop of ink. A currant in the sugar dish, he models in the
    painted flowers, black eye
of Susan, blunt thorn — he delights in my decadence,

the slippery floor, tiles, and stairs haunted with illness: my sensual life
    and his intersect.
He comes on the wing of another spring, in slicks of grey water, the
    pendant sun.

to navigate what is unknown to me, patiently, he regards the chrysalis of
    skin that envelops

the arched veins. Incurious and constant, he is used to waiting for the
modest blush, the rustle of disrobing

the hush. Of silks unfolding, of gossamer veils drawn as tenderly as
breath, from the fluent sea
of *one blood made of two*, the sweetness of his pestilent kiss.

Ambrosia

To thrust all that life under your tongue!

— Anne Sexton

There is always the smell of chocolate, the rich dark swirl and I
separate his wildflower curls when he sleeps:
    Stephen only stayed for moments. Moonlight spooned into our bed,
his red cross grazed my lips, I tasted cherries, his

innocent hand in the night road, calling me — *o la paloma blanca*,
    the radio played this
and he smiled, his mouth

the cranberries we stir into the copper vessels, their skin splits and
    offers bitter fruit.

He became restless: *the guy wanted to leave and I didn't want him to leave.*

A heart-shaped box, the candies are moss-green; I have held on to this
    too long. Anger hot
enough to incinerate each scalloped chocolate I fold into gold foil and twist

his head around, it breaks, I crush his throat with a metal paddle (stolen
from the factory, sweetness is only mine to steal),

wrap his confectionary body into plastic bags, and then retrieve it.

To kiss the rigid wrists and neck that belong to me, sledgehammer
smashes each bone into crystals, stars entombed in stalks of grass.

My first love affair still glitters, when I am here

scattering starlets of cleaning powder on the tile floor, my orange
    coveralls the moon that
tempered him,

by the trees and streetlights, his semaphore fingers spelling Jeffrey, Jeffrey,
for he creeps,

when the first blow reaches my face, I have already retreated. Into
    romance, the rapture.
I held them close

all that life under my tongue, unyielding in my arms, their hollow
    eyes like truffles in cream,
looking back at me.

As a child, I would preserve insects in formaldehyde, dragonflies,
    spiders, a praying mantis.
I fall to my knees in a glaze of pain and remember entreating them,
    don't leave me,
don't leave me please, and what I read,

what I read today: *In those days shall men seek death and shall not*
    find it. My eyes close
like gilded paper, and I find it and

death, my only lover, does not leave.

among the highest bliss

when to thy haunts two kindred spirits flee

— John Keats

The solitude that pursues me has prevailed. Insistent, inexhaustible —
there is an urgency in ending, friendship that has come to sicken me,
what must remain unsaid.

My grandmother, who lies on her bed afternoons with the curtains
    drawn, playing
Casta Diva, has always lived with loss. A blue jewellery box, where a
    tiny ballerina spins
in a net skirt, her daughters:

Robed in the long friends, the dark veins of their mother.

She tells me, I have nothing to dream about anymore. Something
    that aches each day,
the red shoes unseen beneath the latch.

        James is asleep in the other room; once, a circle of flowers fell
and crowned him there. Sleeping, steadily, farther away. He will
be gone when the summer begins

when the sun lights the dry earth where *lilacs last in dooryard bloom'd,*
we plot our separation and let it lie. Fallow, a grief I cannot comprehend,
    or speak of.

My fault — I thought of solitude among the highest bliss, sublimation

heartless men circle me
                they are like sharks (drawn to blood)

a frightened woman said. I helped her home and waited for someone
    to let her inside,
returning late at night and James comes to the door, barely awake.

He has left the telephone by the pillow, if I need him, I need him —

I am swallowing solitude like nightshade; the night we met he said to
me, you stab yourself. And erased the wound, for seven years.

My passionate hatred, undone. With quiet love, his moderate eyes
    closed the day he looked
through the window and saw the sun. Listening: *you don't know what you
    mean to me,*

Watching him unfold, I would ache with fear if he died —

I cover these terrors with fabrication, that it is natural to fall apart,
    flesh from
bone, two spirits arise, severed from each other.

One, as pure as pearl, watches as the other diminishes,

and reaches, once again, for the knife.

After Illness

February returns — a ribbon of pink, a paper wand sealed in ice. Blue
star, a girl in violet tulle and diamante glitter brocades her little bodice.

Pain, my familiar, retreats like the bursts of light that radiate the sky,
at times
a *galaxy of signifiers* arises. Erasing what is liminal, the white lip of snow,

sheer slips of opal, enveloping the earth below.

He moves between these lines — *the individual* — in a crown of fire.
Religion as sacrifice, to hold
the white bird, bind its wings in wire,

and slit its throat. I would draw him closer in a ritual of purity, what I
did not know.

He came to me in violence and romance. How this winter ceremony
descends — gangsters
fall in midnight's alley; children in altar gowns, their necks are slight
white feathers,

each tendon sliced as blood lilts — *Ave Maria*, songs of love. A serenade

in an empty room. The Vietnamese proprietor assembling mirrored
lights and monitors,
he sang, *I was dreaming of the past*. His hair white with sleeplessness,
numinous dreams.

His vertebrae abrading, spineless, he reveals his horror of himself —

    at whose sight all the stars Hide their diminished heads.

The infernal serpent's voice of sulphur and liquid pearl. Rises beneath
the red lights where
we have coiled like snakes alight with diamonds. I slither toward the
hands that will scratch in
trident scars,

the small of my back, at once, asleep. I have been desperately tired,
and he irons this sickness from me in smooth circles.

On a bed of flowers, a pattern of vines and berries. Trace the angry
    letters raised on his flesh,
the ashen clouds, his beauty corrupted, still luminous

as angels are. I must reveal my own dreams in time.

Betrayal, a glacial half-slip, the chill of her fingers breaking into
    blossom, the ice an apparition
the blade divides.

The blue line that creates spheres, defense. His face mutable, implores
    me to assist him.
Afraid of grief, he offers his heart. Creased and ephemeral, it begins
    to discolour the snow

where I have passed, at last, the spirits uncovered. Meaningless stars
without radiance, a metonym, faithless —

the pallor that comes after illness, after its first feverish blush.

Eleven Fortune Cookies
(tears falling down your pretty cheeks)

tears you cannot hide and tears you cannot keep

You will meet a man whose hair stands on end when he shakes it; his
    shower curtain is the Raft
of the Medusa, pink and yellow sails. This **introduction will alter your
    plans**.

He will send you **a letter or paper of great significance**, asking you to
    meet him at midnight,
where heroin girls dance in little steps in

ruby slippers, your emerald dress and garnet hair. His important
    hands circle your waist and you
sigh: **you're in good mood to explore new horizons**. There is a taste
    in his mouth, for amber

and amber and ice. His sophistication will excite you, the razor-pleats,
    the red bordeaux
he makes small fires, an elegant felon who alludes to plans you will
    make. The night sea pared
and spiked with stars, **marriage may bring you wealth**.

He will call rarely but **you have a fortunate sign**. His breath, his
    designs assemble in tea
leaves, a cartomancy you will contrive, prophesying that

the sunlight breaks through the darkest clouds soon. He will pull you
    into his arms, insisting
that he is both *filled with rage* and devotion.

Someone will threaten suicide; **life is short**. He will walk the floor,
    retrieving pictures, agitated,
resting in a circlet against your chest. Where your heart beats like rain
    on a tin roof; he will
flush and cry, tears falling

down his pretty cheeks. **Good advice is never followed.** You will cry as
well, because he is angry, you will say, don't yell at me, don't —

He will say that he didn't mean to hurt you. **The less one speaks,** the
    more silence comes to simulate love.
My father seldom spoke, he will say. Stillness, that quickens the blood
    and you are ashamed

that he left you. **Humility is a sign** of illness; you will remember that
    you thought of Bliss.
As leaves break from moonlit trees, and cold white pears tremble on
    their branches, you will turn
when I am leaving, spilling passion

flowers in my mouth. **You will have to go after what you want.**
    Absorbed in the immaculate
handkerchief you keep pressed and at hand, for error, for accident,
    what you cannot hide
and cannot keep.

Thirteen Ghosts

He overlooked me
all night. Slinging cocktails and
then — he pulled my hair.

One red curl, that had
escaped the rest, the flame lock
latched for seven years.

In the morning, he
combed my wet hair and we sat
by the sun, playing

*please don't let on that
you knew me when* — gold in his
fingers, his glass of

single malt — he shakes
in his sleep, bats stalking mice
blood phlox on the walls.

Nights he disappeared,
comes home drenched in rain water,
my Lear — *that mongrel,*

he strays and returns,
with bird bones, claws set in pearl,
tangled slips of poems,

awful stories — his
life on ships and streets, his love
of beauty that is

terrible and pure.
Protecting me with this, his
shadow resilience,

he waits by my bed,
my baby is gone, catkin
in a cloud of blood

The moon's firing up,
he writes, pulling him to shore,
far from my light house

he goes. Clean, serene:
God grant me the wisdom, to
accept the things I

cannot change. To fill
his hands with change, the ready
hope, my ceaseless love.

Calla, Lily

all the old knives
that have rusted in my back, I drive in yours

— Adrienne Rich

I have made an art of isolation — listen to songs and my languid cat
swoons: *this is the end so why pretend and let it linger on.* I think of
heroin,

like someone in love, the desire that underlines this complaint.

Each day someone is gone. The almost lover, whose tears were pearls
    on the half-
shell of my palms, who said he could see stars —

an impression of stars, long after I left him.

Calla listens to this and more. Afraid of accuracy, she offers me remorse. The
    dressing on her
small hands, discoloured with paint.

Bones of fish, raised below the watercolours of the sea. Pure jade,
    rising from the stones,
the stillness

of my likeness, looking past her; one bare shoulder glacial in breakers
    of black,
waves that pitch

in violence against the shore, indifferent, making sounds as unintelligible
    as the secrets between
us; unspoken, they corrupt our gestures,

what was once fluid. Her body pressed against mine in the Latin
    nightclub, where we turned in
lyrical spheres, arms crossed in cruciform. Her mouth vivid against
    my neck.

Lipstick like dragon's blood, I draw away in fear and compassion. To
    remember that we are
bound in flesh and hatred,

her uneasy prophecy. That I would rise, no longer still, merely dangerous.
And break the spell, with the logic that counters art.

The malice that poisons beauty, my rival. Who dreams endlessly of
    loneliness, who makes
sailor hats from squares of paper,

a grace of tasselled pillows, plum wine, seeds tined in clay pots where
    wildflowers grow,
and there is no light

but what is luminous in memory. She and I, lost in a house of illusions
    one bright summer.
We scaled the sides of the impossible floor, and lay helpless. In its soft
    quilted centre,
in the recesses of this awful room,

I would stay there always, I thought, and she reached, tenderly,
    for my hand.

Fetish

*I'm really sick when it comes to socks . . . They're parts of the
combination to the deepest, most secret recesses of my mind.*

— Ted Bundy

It's one of my fantasies —

     a wooden pharmaceutical chest, drawer after drawer, filled with
    socks. In crisp cellophane envelopes, the colours of the sky

at sunset when I sheathe my *attractive feet* in ribs of black with
    yellow bands
and gather my sticks and gloves, the false sling

starched and clean, secured to my shoulder. Later there is a sense of
    sorrow, remorse,
etcetera; I dislike the other field. Dried leaves and disorderly
    scratches, from
branches, her urgent fingernails

the pain in my hands. I soak them in a basin of warm water and admire
each clever finger
    following the even rows, the letters of the law in my own defense.

I object, the girls all looked the same — that girl with money enough to
    fill each drawer
with a ransom of wool and cotton — spinning gold from a wheel,

spinning when I see the part in her dark hair; her eyes are avarice,
    deflecting me.

I would wear my one pair of socks and underwear and rinse them
    in the sink, the sight of them —
deriding me from the shower rod, threadbare

hooked like signs: the police in Pensacola found traces of her hair,
Even there I was buying socks everywhere.

I am too fine for this, I want to lay out my affluence in sleek pairs,

have her lie among the elastic and silk, like a daisy, *It makes me sad
     because I've never seen*
such — such beautiful socks before.

I imagine it is someone else, tearing their bodies apart, their skin
     in his teeth,

the bite mark that is my undoing, the distinctive curve of poverty: I said
that they were pinned up every night,

I did not mention they were red — they left pale blood-pools on the
     enamel, the white
expanse of their ruined thighs;

*I always felt that I would have really made it if I had all the socks and
underwear I could ever use,*

if I could tear this from one girl or another, her fault.

And somehow find the ecstasy (her last breath pulled slowly from her
     throat), hidden
in the secret recesses,

the deepest pangs —

     I had to restructure my life, from the beginning, I was always so cold.
It may have affected me, alight with fever, I slip her over me.

She is argent, the sheen of the *fleshings*
    folded together, lip to toe like rose petals in my bed,
my bed of roses.

Amaryllis

Let go,
please, your heart is not that strong

— Neil Eustache

You can't miss me, he said. And I waited for him at the long wooden
     table, absorbed
in a cooking show; venison wrapped in cabbage leaves,

the green armature. I have learned to protect myself from strangers; I
     write messages on cocktail
napkins, *leave me alone, leave me.*

He walks toward me, his face dispassionate, one tooth absent, a cryptic
     space like superstition.
The region between ladders, where spirits gather. And evanesce above
     crossed fingers,

souls retreating from faith.

The *beauty that does not die* at the centre of his terrible stories. The
     stranger who caressed him
as he slept, who lost his car keys and desire, William retrieves himself

in memory and ceremony. Smoothing the earth of his mother's grave,
     his basement room, where
he lay, coronated in candles, his mother's voice.

The violence that marks his hands, a broken finger, unspeakable
     fights — *be a man*, he brands
this on his back with hot wire. With irony, because he is tender, without.

He draws a map for me of Kamloops, a sepulchre with a circle, an
     arrow: where I come from,
where I have been. Bereft, without belief, he offers me charity. Reaches to
     me and lifts my
abject face;

we will meet in accident. To plan a mink farm, there are minks loose
    everywhere, what we
refuse to kill;

at the *Lanterne Verde*, in an unravelled sweater, a shadow of grey and
    lichen-green,

to see the gardens that are cased in glass.

The day he left, we looked at one-eyed fish in the leaden stream. The
    air was sleepy, as sultry
as the silk-red amaryllis

that bent their narrow blooms in sorrow.

He left me with this, and something else — perennial, his counsel. Your
    bones are
made this way. Emerald stalks, between flower, resisting loss, secure
    and certain

in the shelter, of the green house.

all my seasick sailors

Sly and second-sighted, my friends have abandoned ship. Rats,
     escaping in small grey
lifeboats, their annular tails turn the tide, their lambent eyes, like the
     moon, dictate its flow.
The violinist plays *Autumn* as the masts unfold, water lilies in the
     pitch of the sea.

A message in semaphore, what I have always longed to know — to stand
     by the stern, and
with courage, let go. Nostalgia's poison

love spreads out like a sheaf of photographs, memory without blood,
     a fluked anchor,
undone. The line that breaks when the storm comes, the truth that
     sailors know:
red skies without delight,

a bad sign. To navigate you must know where you are going, with an
     exact chart,
pin-stuck with ellipses. Accidents, typhoon, the fibrous stakes of sea
     monsters, the diamond icecaps,

miracles that have changed course, carved passages into the new
     worlds, where sailors
arise. In white militia,

letters come like gulls flat on the crest of waves, infatuation coursing,
     like a science of chaos,

they appear in envelopes of ice, intermittent ghosts — to remind me
     that love is spectral,
unforeseen.

The rapids were turbulent toward the Asian corridor, sailing into
     Lachine. It is China, after all.
Rare and fragile, esteemed from a great distance,

protected in shelf-ice.

I touch this china from rim to stem, and feel its raised flowers,
　　brought to me from the ocean's
floor. *In spite of the danger*, the mariners have garlanded the stingray
— as the lashings narrowed,

they retrieved me from the wreck.

Geography
for Daniel Jones

i. Love

To see him I would walk to Grace, past the windows of hooks — calves
    with their brown-paper
gowns, lobsters sinking in kale-green tanks. Their premonitory eyes
    are flat dead stones.

Ephemera designed to obscure memory, glass jars of seeds, vines of
    purple grapes.
He spoke to me with difficulty; admissions I cannot remember, but
    his hands,
his lips are still

stained with violet. I meant to say I loved him; I did not.

I came to Grace, measuring his loathing for things esoteric to him —
irregular grammar, wild dogs, all vegetables — some terrible dream of
    red cabbage,
its radiant veins and leaves

            suffocating him, that his bones and blood would flourish,
that he may live, that he may

continue to suffer my own sadness with a silence particular to him.
    A silence I did not know was
fraught with anger, night terrors: a cerement of spider filaments,
    their slender malice.

The small parameters he drew for safety. We walked within these lines
without deviation, encompassed by stars, he could almost breathe, he
    could chart
the fever of hatred that spikes as it turns inward

unsettling him. I have seen the artifacts and ruins,
his derelict bathtub — there was a drama there, his first death.

It is arduous, approaching grace. You must continue, trace the narrow
    lines of its map, and be
prepared. To draw the blade neatly,

divide your wrists into continents. Rivers are created, tributaries,
    fault-lines —
geography's red and blue relief, where forgiveness lies remote
and uncharted.

ii. Anger

Anger comes between us — the street's topography, black branches
    stitch its grey
surface, an arbitrary parallel. I am superstitious when I pass his window,
the blue light where he works, a faint plume of smoke in the
    darkened panes.

Anger that is fatal if it is unspoken, anaesthesia without surgery,
    cyanide tablets in mid-
fall: the brittle leaves break as I gather them seedpods spin

pollen wraiths, wasp-fossils in glass — the time he removed its bite
    with iodine and I
cried, his hands extracting venom and now
erasing me, plotting my demise. The tragedian that he is, that I am

performing the final act *(The weight of this sad time we must obey)* in
    Kensington Market.
Where palm trees and impatiens were there are skeletal cats,
crates of decadent vegetables, there is John

repelling me and I write, later: *how did I not see his hatred*, the sable leaves
of artichokes unfolding, poison at the centre.

I withdraw from the sting, *peripeteia* — his sudden ruin a tiresome
    convention.
He was capable of cruelty; he was meticulous, theatrical. His shaven
    head a courtesy,
facilitating the coroner's scalpel

the measure of the radius (once an aurora of pain), faint tremors,
the uneasy crown of fury, relinquished. I passed by him, several times,
    my head bowed
in fear and contempt.

Until the day I looked again, where I imagined he was, his door closed
    that he would open to
me, what he had offered me. Light, clarifying the pearl, the cautious
    fracture that
injures the membrane. He set out cups and saucers, expecting me;
    I ascended

the perilous steps toward him. *I miss you*, I thought, as the sun
    streaked like an urchin, and
punished his delicate heart.

iii. Loss

He came home on a Friday, sick, and stayed in the back room with
    bowls of soup
and napkins. A crumpled blanket, a small writing pad. *Frog Moon*
    underlined,
the door locked, bad news

collected elsewhere. Things are shrinking, this one room
the snow drifts, a border of chrysanthemum, encompassing
the enclosure, the necropolis: *Il Gatto Nero*, the Golden Wheat —

where we met and you spilled your coffee — happy to see me, sweet
friend I had forgotten

your rare, infectious bliss.

Lost, you left signs I read backwards: *a day in early winter without plan,
without direction, incomprehensible and monstrous,*

you left nothing, stacks of empty boxes, no ventilation in the plastic bag
that smothers the death rattle. You left

and were carried down the stairs, in the indifferent hands of the ushers,
rubber gloves closing your eyes, yellow police-tape pushed
through the bannisters,

carnival. One Easter we watched this from your window, the stations
    of the cross,
the figure of Veronica, her ghost-veil pressed to her white robe, passing

as religious, I solemnly unpeel the 2 from your door, it leaves a
    little space.
There are emerald draperies in your windows now, I see the lush
    leaves
of *monsteria* plants.

The new number that is fastened there. It is slight, a slip of paper that
    will be torn away
when the winds begin again, when the ice and early darkness come.
    To fall in reverence,
what you alone discovered —

Grace.

Acknowledgements

I want to thank, as always, my family and friends, with much love. Particular thanks and love to Tony Burgess.

I am indebted to Chris Dewdney, Michael Holmes, David Trinidad, Michael Turner, and Martha Sharpe for assistance tendered.

And I wish to acknowledge the inspiring — Jeffery Conway, Al Purdy, Stuart Ross, David Keyes, Liz Renzetti, Clint Burnham, Moira Farr, Guy Lawson, Jerome Burgess, Handsome Ned, The Ministry of Love, John Berryman, James Wright's "Blessing," and Jim Wafer's *The Taste of Blood*.

The support of the Canada Council, the Ontario Arts Council, and the City of Toronto through the Toronto Arts Council is gratefully acknowledged.

Michael Holmes's *james I wanted to ask you* (1994) quoted on page 1 with permission from the author and ECW Press.

Quote on page 4 from Daniel Jones, "In Various Restaurants," from *The People One Knows* (The Mercury Press, Stratford, Ontario: 1994). Used by permission.

Excerpts from "Live" (on page 6 here) and "Wanting to Die" (on page 35 here), from *Live or Die* by Anne Sexton. Copyright © 1996 by Anne Sexton. Reprinted by permission of Houghton Mifflin Co. All rights reserved.

Jeffery Conway's correspondence quoted on page 7 by permission from the author.

Al Purdy's "On Being Human" from *Naked with Summer in Your Mouth* (McClelland & Stewart: 1994) quoted on page 24 with permission of the author.

Quote on page 27 from Theodore Roethke, "In a Dark Time," *The Collected Poems of Theodore Roethke* (Bantam Doubleday Dell Publishing Group, Inc.). Used by permission.

Tony Burgess's "The Lice Age" from *Nob Swimming* (1992) quoted on page 44 with permission from the author and Pink Dog Press.

Excerpt on page 31 from *Anne Sexton: A Self-Portrait in Letters*, edited by Linda Gray Sexton and Lois Ames. Copyright © 1977 by Linda Gray Sexton and Loring Conant, Jr., executors of the will of Anne Sexton. Reprinted by permission of Houghton Mifflin Co. All rights reserved.

The lines on page 45 from "Snapshots of a Daughter-in-Law," copyright © 1993, 1963 by Adrienne Rich from *Collected Early Poems:*